KIDDING AROUND

San Francisco

A YOUNG PERSON'S GUIDE TO THE CITY

ROSEMARY ZIBART

ILLUSTRATED BY JANICE ST. MARIE

John Muir Publications

Santa Fe, New Mexico

For my father, who interested me in history, and for my mother, who has always helped me write.

Special thanks to Andrew and Frances Victor Zibart for their assistance in photo research.

A big hug from Janice to Resa, whose presence can be seen throughout the book.

John Muir Publications, P.O. Box 613, Santa Fe, NM 87504

First edition. Second printing

Photo credits: pp. 24, 32—San Francisco Public Library; p. 42—Nancy Rodger ("A.M. Lightning," The Exploratorium); p. 47—Joe Samberg (Oakland Museum, Cowell Hall of California History); p. 50—Richard Heeger/CMMC (California Marine Mammal Center); p. 54—San Francisco Public Library; p. 56—Sharon Risedorph (Esprit Kids, Valley Fair, San Jose, Calif.)

Library of Congress Cataloging-in-Publication Data

Zibart, Rosemary.
    Kidding around San Francisco: a young person's guide to the city
/ Rosemary Zibart: illustrated by Janice St. Marie.—1st ed.
        p. cm.
    Includes index.
    Summary: A guidebook to San Francisco for children eight years and older, informing them about the sights and events of that beautiful city.
    ISBN 0-945465-23-8
    1. San Francisco (Calif.)—Description—Guide-books—Juvenile literature. [1. San Francisco (Calif.)—Description—Guides.]
I. St. Marie, Janice. ill. II. Title.
F869.S33Z53   1989
917.94'610453—dc 19   88-43535
                                                        CIP

Typeface: Trump Medieval
Typesetter: Copygraphics, Santa Fe, New Mexico
Designer: Joanna V. Hill
Printer: Eurasia Press
Printed in Singapore

Distributed to the book trade by:
W.W. Norton & Company, Inc.
New York, New York

Contents

1. On Your Mark, Get Set . . .GO! / 4
2. Put Yourself on the Map / 7
3. Put Yourself in the Picture / 10
4. Adventures in Time / 12
5. Golden Gate Park / 16
6. Close Neighborhoods / 20
7. Fisherman's Wharf / 25
8. Two Island Escapes / 29
9. The Hills — 42 Ups and Downs / 31
10. Clowning Around and Carousels / 34
11. Bridging the Bay / 36
12. Parks Aplenty / 37
13. Special Attractions (for Science Nuts, History Buffs, and Animal Lovers) / 41
14. Hey Gang, I'm HUNGRY! / 52
15. Super Shopping Stops / 55
16. Celebrating Round the Year / 58
17. Fortune Cookies and Farewell / 61

Index of Points of Interest / 62

1. Get Ready, Get Set...GO!

re you ready for this trip? What are you thinking about? Some typical pretrip questions are:

What should I wear? Will it be cold or hot?

What should I bring? A camera, a backpack, a full piggy bank.

Where will we eat? What will we see? Who will we meet?

Thinking ahead about this trip will help you make the most of your time. It's obvious that whether you have one day, one week, or one month, there's not enough time to do everything.

Also, what you want to do (or where you want to eat) may be different from what Mom, Dad, or brothers and sisters want. How will these choices be made? How will everyone get a chance to voice their opinion without squashing someone else's desires. You're all together on this vacation and for it to be a success, everyone should have a *super* time—both fun and inspiring.

But how can you figure out what you want to do? And how can you figure out what is possible to do in one day? That's where a guidebook like this one is useful. Reading it before you leave (or on the way) will help you make a plan.

To make an itinerary, first read up on the possibilities. Make your own top choices, and then ask others what they most care about. Write in this guidebook—star or circle the special, not-to-be-missed items. Mark up the maps—what is close to what? Where can you go in one day? Will it be easier to use public transportation, walk, or go by car?

These are decisions normally left to grown-ups. And, of course, your parents will make the final decisions about how to get somewhere or how many places you can afford to visit. But let's face it, parents usually have their hands full at vacation time. They'd probably appreciate your help!

Keep in mind that not everything will turn out as you plan. But planning can save you and your family a few hassles. And you can be sure to take in a few incredible, awesome, *something to tell the folk's back home about* experiences.

The plan for a trip is called an itinerary.

Turn to the next page for a sample itinerary.

Trip Itinerary
Here's space to write
down what you and your
family want to do. Use a
pencil as this could
change.
My top choices:
1.
2.
3.
4.
5.

Mom's choices:
1.
2.
3.

Dad's choices:
1.
2.
3.

Others:
1.   1.
2.   2.
3.   3.

Also, don't worry, because it's 99 percent sure that whatever you decide to do, you'll have a fabulous trip, *especially in San Francisco!*

Many people consider San Francisco to be the most beautiful city in the world. Because of its beauty, its good climate, and the opportunity for work, San Francisco has attracted people from all over the world. And they have brought their own cultures and ways of living. So visiting San Francisco is a little like taking a mini-tour of the world.

San Francisco itself is a special, unique, unforgettable place. It combines a wide mix of people and great natural beauty with a sense of fun and adventure.

San Franciscans like to have a good time. They love to eat well, dress with originality, and celebrate. They have hosted two world fairs just to show the rest of the world how to have a good time. Almost every day you'll find a fair, festival, or parade in some part of the city.

Any trip is an opportunity for *adventure.* Adventure requires the courage to take risks. Not risks like hanging from your heels from the Golden Gate Bridge! What it could mean is tasting something completely new. Or exploring a science museum when you thought you only liked art. An adventure is possible whenever you try things out with open eyes and a clear head.

So are you ready? Are you set? LET'S GO!

2. Put Yourself on the Map

The city of San Francisco is on the tip of a 32-mile-long peninsula. To the west, the cold waves of the Pacific Ocean crash on a shore of rocks and sand. To the north is a narrow, deep strip of salt water called the Golden Gate. Through the Golden Gate, strong currents (and tons of water) flow in and out of the huge San Francisco Bay. This bay is one of the largest land-locked (surrounded by land) harbors in the world.

The Bay is 558 square miles. That's 6 miles long and 14 miles at its greatest width. It's mostly shallower than 18 feet, but the channel through the Golden Gate is 381 feet deep.

Explore different ways to travel around the city. **BART** (Bay Area Rapid Transit; 788-BART) travels 71 miles, connecting the city to 25 stations across the Bay. **MUNI** (San Francisco Municipal Railway; 673-MUNI) controls the

*San Francisco population:
712,753
Size: 46 square miles
Can you figure out the density (number of persons) per square mile?*

San Francisco is located at longitude 122 degrees, 31 minutes and latitude 37 degrees, 48 minutes. If you traveled directly around the world, San Francisco would be in the same latitude as Tokyo, Japan, Athens, Greece, Seville, Spain, or Washington, D.C.
The distance between San Francisco and
• Los Angeles is 369 miles
• Seattle is 796 miles
• Honolulu is 2,095 miles
• Hong Kong is 6,044 miles
• Miami is 3,053 miles
• New York City is 2,799 miles
Can you calculate the distance from your home?

cable cars (see chap. 6, Close Neighborhoods), electric buses (trolleys), buses, and the Owl Service (late-night buses). **Ferries** transport you around the Bay.

Use the telephone numbers listed above to get information about the easiest way to get from one place to another.

Of course, foot power works well in this compact city.

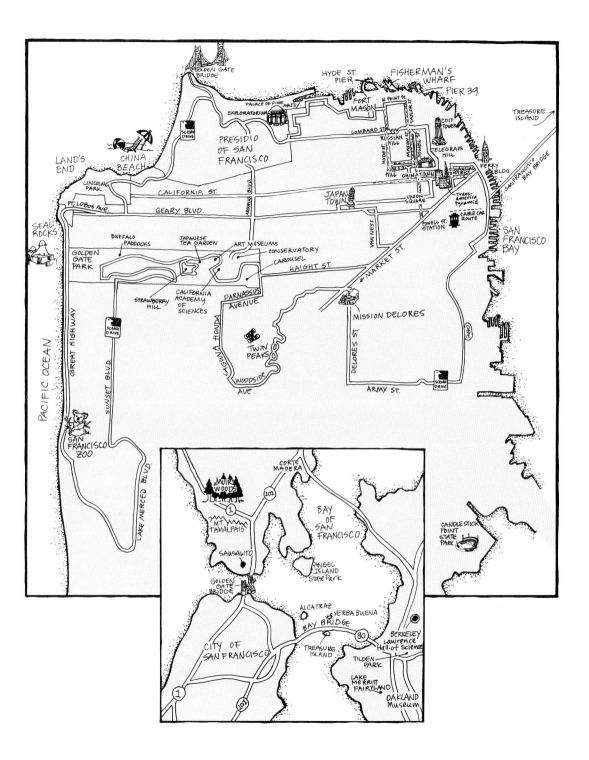

3. Put Yourself in the Picture

I magine standing on a hill so high and steep you could ski to the bottom (if there was any snow). Imagine streets winding up and down like a roller coaster. From perches high and low, glimpse pieces of blue—the choppy blue of the Bay, the shimmering blue of the Pacific, the kite-filled blue sky.

Suddenly, a stiff salty breeze blows your hair. Someone walking past is speaking Italian, Russian, or Japanese. Shop windows tantalize with intriguing treasures. A street musician is playing. *Umm*, something smells outrageously delicious!

Seems like you've made it! Worth the trip? Definitely! But, before you hit the streets, here are some tips about what to wear. Comfortable shoes for walking are, of course, #1 on any trip. Also, aside from blue jeans, you may want to have some nice clothes for eating in restaurants or going to shows. You'll notice that San Franciscans enjoy being casual, but they also like dressing up.

As for the weather, will it be hot or cold? That's not easy to answer. In San Francisco you can sometimes freeze in summer and enjoy

Breathe deeply. If you smell somthing unusual— fragrant but not sweet— look around for some tall trees with shaggy bark and grayish green leaves. You may have caught a whiff of eucalyptus. This exotic tree was imported long ago from Australia. Eucalyptus thrives in the San Francisco area as do trees from South Africa, New Zealand, and even the Canary Islands.

warm sunshine in winter. Not only does the weather change in one hour but the temperature can be very different from one part of the city to another.

Usually the weather is not very hot (above 75 degrees) or very cold (below 45 degrees). The reason it stays moderate is its natural air conditioner, *fog*. Only two or three warm days are needed to draw cool, moist breezes in from the ocean. A white cloud swells over the land, hiding the sun. The fog may last from a few hours to a few weeks. But finally the sun evaporates the drops of moisture and sunshine again appears.

There are only two seasons: wet and dry. The rains occur from October to May.

Plants definitely dig this climate. San Francisco is in the Mediterranean Climate Zone (like the countries France, Italy, and Spain which border the Mediterranean Sea). More kinds of plants can grow in this zone than in any other.

You'll see flowers everywhere. Red and yellow nasturtiums grow like weeds. Calla lilies grow wild. And jade plants that elsewhere only grow inside in pots look like funny little trees in front yards.

Now, you've arrived, but how did San Francisco come to be here? Get that answer by going back in time.

Koalas both live in and eat eucalyptus. See for yourself at the Koala Crossing in the San Francisco Zoo (see chap. 13, Special Attractions).

11

4. Adventures in Time

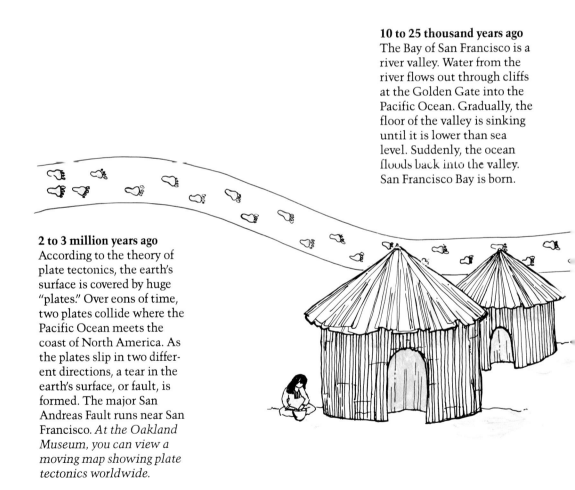

10 to 25 thousand years ago
The Bay of San Francisco is a river valley. Water from the river flows out through cliffs at the Golden Gate into the Pacific Ocean. Gradually, the floor of the valley is sinking until it is lower than sea level. Suddenly, the ocean floods back into the valley. San Francisco Bay is born.

2 to 3 million years ago
According to the theory of plate tectonics, the earth's surface is covered by huge "plates." Over eons of time, two plates collide where the Pacific Ocean meets the coast of North America. As the plates slip in two different directions, a tear in the earth's surface, or fault, is formed. The major San Andreas Fault runs near San Francisco. *At the Oakland Museum, you can view a moving map showing plate tectonics worldwide.*

1579

Sir Francis Drake, the English sea captain, probably never sees the Bay but he does land nearby. Miwok Indians think his pale, bearded men are spirits coming from the Isle of the Dead.

1769

Don Gaspar de Portal discovers the Bay of San Francisco by accident. He was looking for Monterey Bay.

200 to 8,000 years ago

Native Americans live in villages surrounding the Bay. *For a description of their culture, see chapter 13, Special Attractions for History Buffs, Oakland Museum.*

WRONG WAY!

1776

Spanish settlers arrive overland from Mexico. They build a fort (the Presidio) and a church (Mission Dolores). They call their little village Yerba Buena, which means sweet grass (the herb mint) in Spanish.

No trace of the fort remains. Its location is **Presidio Park** *on a bluff overlooking the Golden Gate channel.*

Mission Dolores *is still standing. It was first constructed of mud brick walls (adobe) and hand-carved timber tied together with leather thongs.*

1846

An American ship, the *S.S. Portsmouth* sails into the Bay. Yankees (as the Spanish called them) raise the "Stars and Stripes" and call the town San Francisco.

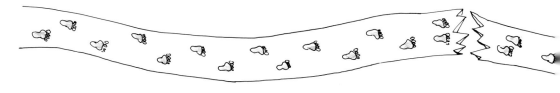

1848

Gold is discovered at Sutter's Mill, 150 miles from San Francisco. Ships and wagons from all over the world arrive, loaded with men wanting to strike it rich. They go ashore, buy a pick, bucket, and shovel and head after their dream.

5:13 a.m., April 18, 1906

On the night of April 17, animals began acting strangely. Horses were neighing loudly and stamping their hooves. No one understood why until the next morning at 5:13. Suddenly, the ground begins moving in giant waves! Beds slide across the floor, furniture topples, schoolbooks fall to the floor. It's a tremendous earthquake.

The noise is like thousands of violins—all playing at once and out of tune. The earthquake only lasts 48 seconds. But the disaster is just beginning!

Most wooden buildings survive the quake. But gas and water lines are broken. Fires start in cracked chim-

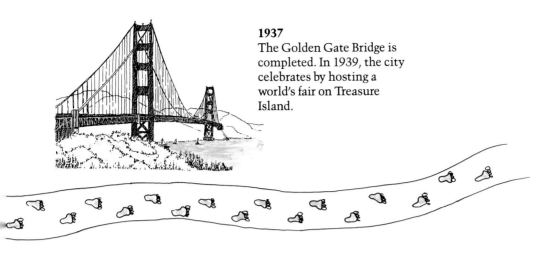

1937
The Golden Gate Bridge is completed. In 1939, the city celebrates by hosting a world's fair on Treasure Island.

neys and broken furnaces. And there is no way to get water to put them out.

The fire grows bigger and spreads from street to street. It can only be stopped by dynamiting buildings in its path. One beautiful building after another is destroyed.

After three days, smoke and cinders remain. Five square miles of the city are destroyed. People sleep in tents in the city parks while the city is rebuilt. Even camping in the parks, San Franciscans are determined to have a good time. They sing and play music under the stars.

It is no wonder that a symbol for San Francisco is the Phoenix—the mythical bird that is born and reborn in fire.

1967
"Love-in's" become popular for "flower children'" living in the Haight District of San Francisco. Their message: "Make love not war."

15

5. Golden Gate Park

ith only *one* day in San Francisco, where should you go? **Golden Gate Park** is a good choice. Whether you roller skate, jog, ride horseback, or drive through, it's gorgeous. Plus there's lots to do.

Head first for the **California Academy of Sciences, Steinhart Aquarium,** and **Morrison Planetarium**. They're in the same building for one admission price.

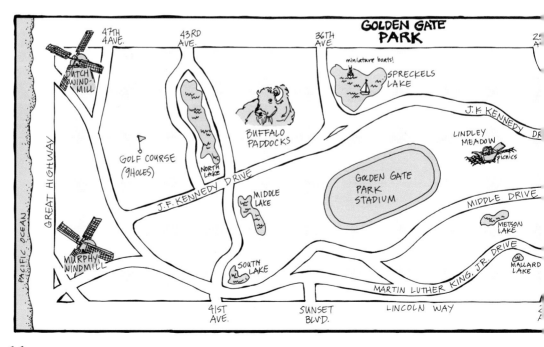

At the aquarium, you'll pass through a hallway lined with dozens of aquariums. Each shows a different marine habitat. Walk on, and you'll be at eye level with dolphins gracefully swimming in an underwater tank.

Then, you can reach into the Touching Tidepool to examine clams, sea snails, starfish, and other shellfish. Above you, sea bass, tuna, sharks, and other big fish constantly circle in a 100,000-gallon Fish Roundabout.

Near the Aquarium is the **Wattis Hall of Man**. This anthropology exhibit shows how humans in different cultures live. You'll visit places far from telephones or television. Observe daily life with an Eskimo family in the cold Arctic. Then study survival in the dry desert camp of an Australian Aborigine.

You can stargaze in the **Morrison Planetarium**. For information on daily shows like "Star Death—Birth of Black Holes," call 221-5100.

Another attraction is 21 penguins that line up for meals at 11:30 a.m. and 4:00 p.m. daily.

For laughs, stop in The Far Side of Science—a roomful of cartoons by Gary Larson.

A small buffalo herd grazes near Spreckles Lake. Their ancestors were saved when buffalo in the wild were disappearing.

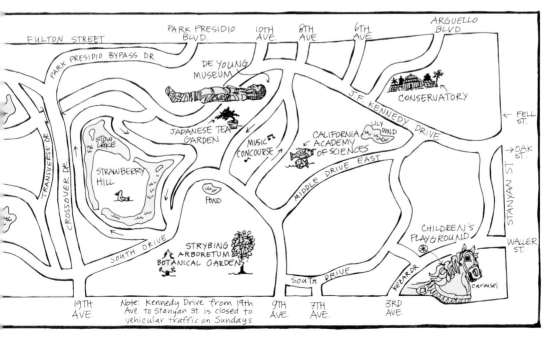

Did you used to think art museums were boring? Check out the **M. H. DeYoung Memorial Museum**. From pharoah's golden statues to modern paintings, it's anything but dull. There's an Alaskan totem pole and a real Egyptian mummy—guess how old it is.

A free class, "Doing and Viewing Art," for ages 7-12 is held Saturdays, 10:30 a.m.-12:00 noon (advance registration *not* required). "How Art Is Made" (known as HAM) shows how artists make a sculpture, paint a landscape, or create in other media. HAM is for kids and adults on Saturdays at 1:00 p.m.

The **Japanese Tea Garden** is only a few steps from the DeYoung Museum. Yet passing through the hand-carved gate is like jumping across an ocean. You'll see dwarf bonsai trees, a bridge as high as it is long (you have to climb *up* to cross *over* it), pools of magical goldfish, and a tall bright gold and red pagoda or temple.

Your family can rent a boat on doughnut-shaped **Stow Lake**. Or on weekends, you can watch miniature boats that sail or motor across **Spreckles Lake.** Also look for the **Conservatory of Flowers** (called the Crystal Palace)—a beautiful glass greenhouse.

Can you believe this wonderful flowering park used to be windy sand dunes? People laughed at the idea of making a park here. Fortunately, the first park superintendent had a different idea. The story goes that one night his horse was feeding on a bag of barley and knocked it over. The barley sprouted, so the superintendent planted more. Soon, the sturdy barley roots kept the soil from blowing away. Thousands of trees and bushes were added — now everyone enjoys the results.

6. Close Neighborhoods

San Francisco is like a patchwork quilt. In each neighborhood, people have their favorite stores, restaurants, and playgrounds.

Also notice the size and shape of buildings. Architects and artists love this city because there's such variety. Old and new blend. There are skyscrapers next to many 2- to 4-story buildings.

You can walk to two famous San Francisco neighborhoods or travel by **cable car**, the only *moving* National Historic Monument.

There are three cable lines. For a real roller coaster ride, climb aboard the **Powell-Hyde Line**. It zigzags up and over both Nob Hill and Russian Hill, ending at the Aquatic Park. Another exciting trip is the **Powell-Mason Line,** which climbs Nob Hill before cruising down to Fisherman's Wharf. Your third choice is the **California Line**—kind of a flat ride.

Line up the day's activities with one of the cable car routes. Students pay only 75 cents. And one ticket lets you ride several hours, getting on or off. (Check with the conductor for the time limit on your ticket—then stick it in your pocket.)

When Andrew Hallidie was a boy, he saw a terrible accident. Horses, pulling a wagon filled with people, slipped near the top of a hill. The heavy car dragged the horses back down, and one horse broke its leg. Hallidie swore he could invent something better and in 1873 he did: the cable car.

A good place to hop aboard is Union Square, a lovely green square ringed with fancy department stores—great for window shopping!

From Union Square, ride only three blocks to Bush Street. Climb off and look up! Why *up*? Because you've arrived in **Chinatown.** Many roofs here are curved up at each corner. The street lights look like Chinese lanterns, and the phone booths are bright oriental red.

There isn't a wall around Chinatown, but there is a gate. By walking to the intersection of Bush Street and Grant Avenue, you'll discover a two-level archway guarded by two dragons with open jaws. Never fear, they are welcoming you into this busy, fascinating area.

To see the original "Hallidie's folly" and other antique cars, visit the **Cable Car Barn** *(on the corner of Washington and Mason streets, 474-1887).*

Chinatown is the largest Chinese community (over 120,000 people) outside China. Many Chinese came here during the 1848 gold rush. They crossed the Pacific, hoping to strike it rich and return to China. Not everyone hit the jackpot and earned enough for passage back to China. So they stayed in San Francisco and fished or sold fresh vegetables to earn a living.

Thousands more Chinese were lured to this country to work on the railroad linking the East to the West Coast. They worked long hours, 7 days a week, for $30.00 a month. Once the railroad was complete, many Chinese settled in San Francisco, calling their new home Gum Sahn (Golden Hills).

Grant Avenue is the main route through Chinatown. Shop windows everywhere are jammed with the unexpected. Inside herb shops, unusual odors waft from bags and jars.

In food stores, you'll spy stacks of dried and pickled fish— from shrimp to sharks fins. Salted

*To explore Chinese culture, visit the **Chinese Cultural Center**, 750 Kearney, 3rd floor of the Holiday Inn, 986-1822.*

ducks from Hong Kong hang in golden rows, so flat they look starched and pressed. (In fact, on the menu, they're called *pressed duck*.)

Whoever isn't shopping seems to be eating. Whether or not Chinese food is new to you, Chinatown offers the chance to try something different—like *dim sum*, which means "heart's delight." These little steamed or fried pastries are offered from a cart that comes to your table. You can start out ordering one or two and add on as long as you're hungry.

In the mood for a snack? Check out a Chinese bakery. Its shelves are crowded with cakes, buns, and almond cookies. With a bagful, you could stroll over to **Portsmouth Square** where the American flag was first hoisted in 1846. This spot has been visited by several famous authors such as Jack London, the adventurous author of *Call of the Wild*, and Rudyard Kipling, who wrote *The Jungle Books* and *Just So Stories*. Look for a bronze statue of a ship saluting the

On your way out of Chinatown, why not drop in the **Golden Gate Fortune Cookie Company** *(56 Ross Alley/Washington) and watch fortunes being made.*

Three DiMaggio brothers from North Beach played ball professionally. The best known was "Joltin' Joe." For big league action, visit windy Candlestick Park, home to the San Francisco Forty-niners and the Giants.

seafarer Robert Louis Stevenson, who wrote *Kidnapped* and *Treasure Island*—he also visited this spot.

Ready to cross the border from China to Italy? These two nations are side by side if you walk (or ride the Powell-Hyde Line) north into **North Beach.** Don't worry, you won't need a bathing suit. North Beach hasn't been a real beach for years. It is home to thousands of Americans of Italian ancestry. Italians came here generations ago to fish in the Bay and the Pacific. (And their great-grandchildren's children are still fishing in this area.)

In the 1906 earthquake and fire, Italian families tried desperately to save their homes. They soaked rugs with wine and hung them in front of buildings. It didn't help. Most of North Beach burned down.

But it was quickly rebuilt thanks to Amadeo Peter Giannini and the Bank of Italy. Giannini didn't like the way other banks ignored Italian and other recent immigrants so he started his own. A few days after the earthquake and fire, his bank returned to business with a wooden plank across two barrels. Eventually, the little Bank of Italy became the huge Bank of America.

Now North Beach is popular for Italian bakeries or *pasticcerias* (pronounced pah-steet-sir-rias). These serve an awesome selection of luscious Italian pastries.

Long after the Italians settled in North Beach (that is, in the 1950s), the *beatniks* arrived. They were rebels who wanted to change the values of society. We can learn of their ideas from their music, poetry, and literature.

7. Fisherman's Wharf

his is the end of two cable car lines, yet there's so much to do, you may wish you had started your trip here. You'll find almost everything but fishermen. That includes a lot of *schlock* (the Yiddish word for junk), so watch your coins. Depending on your taste, however, there are many things in the not-to-be-missed category. For example, boating enthusiasts can head straight for the **National Maritime Museum** and **Hyde Street Pier.**

The museum looks like a beached boat (as the architect intended). Inside are miniature replicas of the cutters, clippers, and freighters that sailed or steamed in and out of the Bay during the past 200 years. The walls are decorated with great underwater scenes—murals (wall paintings) on the inside and mosaics (pictures in ceramic tile) on the outside.

You can see the real thing at **Hyde Street Pier.** Here several historic ships are being preserved by the National Park Service.

Climb aboard the **Balclutha**, a square-rigged Cape Horn sailing ship. Built in Scotland, the *Balclutha* first sailed in 1888, carrying wine, coal, and hardware from Europe to San Francisco. Then it returned with California wheat.

People swim at the beach below the National Maritime Museum. In fact, on New Year's Day, members of the Polar Bear Club swim to Alcatraz Island and back. Yikes!

25

Where are the fish at Fisherman's Wharf? They're cooked. Look for the gigantic Dungeness crabs or taste the spicy fish chowder called cioppino (cho-pino).

For quick snacks, buy little paper cups filled with seafood called "walkaway seafood cocktails."

With any fish dinner you'll be served the famous San Francisco sourdough bread.

You can explore the *Balclutha* from prow to stern. Examine the captain's quarters and the tiny cook's galley. Take a turn at the steering wheel while eyeing the compass.

Next check out the ferry ***Eureka***. Before the bridges across the Bay were built, this boat carried thousands of passengers back and forth every day. On board, you can easily imagine what a pleasant trip this was. There's room to stroll on the decks, meet a friend for a cup of tea in the lounge, watch gulls overhead, or study the ship's wake behind. Below deck, you'll see a prime collection of antique automobiles and trucks.

Another ship you can see but not board is the lovely sailing schooner ***Alma***. It carried hay and lumber to ports within the Bay. Also on the pier is a boat-building woodshop where a wooden dinghy is under construction.

Two historic boats are located at different piers. The ***Jeremiah O'Brien*** is the last unchanged survivor of over 2,000 Liberty Ships built during World War II. At Fort Mason you can board this giant ship, which carried troops and supplies throughout the world.

At Pier 45 you can step aboard the submarine, ***Pampanito,*** used during World War II for long-range cruises in the Pacific. Experience its cramped living quarters and view the torpedo arsenal.

From Hyde Street Pier, it's only a few steps to **Ghirardelli** (gear-ar-deli) **Square** and **The Cannery.** Ghirardelli Square was once a cocoa factory. The Cannery used to be—you guessed it—a peach-canning factory. These old brick buildings have been turned into multistory shopping centers.

The Ghirardelli Company is still making chocolate. And wow—what chocolate! Watch it being made in the old-fashioned ice cream parlor on the first level. From dry bean pods it becomes the thick, oozy brown stuff we know and love.

On the third floor of the Cannery is the **San Francisco International Toy Museum** (441-TOYS). Toys from around the world are on display.

At the **American Carousel Museum** (633 Beach St., 928-0550), you'll see a wonderful collection of wooden painted animals. These magical creatures once belonged on merry-go-rounds all over the country. See chapter 10, Clowning Around and Carousels.

Nearby at the **Wax Museum** (145 Jefferson St.,

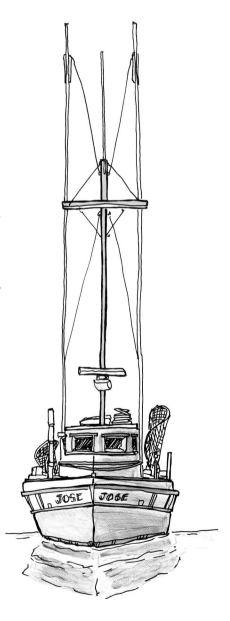

Notice the lovely mermaid fountain in the courtyard of Ghirardelli Square. Musicians, mimes, jugglers, or magicians often perform here.

885-4975), you'll see over 270 celebrities arranged in lifelike scenes. Especially interesting is a model of King Tut's Tomb with its golden treasures.

Close by is the **Haunted Gold Mine** (111 Jefferson St.), full of tricks, mazes, and tunnels.

On the same street you'll find **Ripley's Believe It or Not** (175 Jefferson St., 771-6188). Its exhibits are chock-full of incredible (but true) happenings. If you believe it!

Last but not least is the **Guinness Museum of World Records** (235 Jefferson St., 771-9890). Watch films showing nutty contests like the world's longest domino roll. Measure yourself next to a replica of the tallest human—or try to embrace the fattest.

Pier 39 used to be a broken down wharf. Now it's a mini-shopping mall built over the water. If you hear rumbling noises, they are probably part of a multimedia show called **San Francisco Experience.** Inside its small theater you'll feel the shake and watch the flames from the famous 1906 earthquake and fire.

Also at Pier 39, you can ride a double-decker carousel. Or try out your skills in a video game parlor called **Funtasia**.

Still having a good time? Being a tourist is usually fun but also very, very tiring. Step away from the crowds for a moment . . . breathe deeply. The salty air and view of the water are always refreshing.

For Pier 39 shopping, see chapter 15, Super Shopping Stops.

8. Two Island Escapes

This island was first called Nuestra Senora de los Angeles (Our Lady of the Angels).

To reserve space for camping on Angel Island, call 1-800-446-7275.

eady to leave the crowds at Fisherman's Wharf behind? You can escape to the middle of the Bay where beautiful **Angel Island** awaits. (Buy tickets at Fisherman's Wharf, Pier 43½, the Red and White Fleet [546-2896]. Two trips daily.)

It was named by Lieutenant Don Juan Manuel de Ayala who anchored nearby while making a map of the Bay in 1775. Miwok Indians watched from the island as he worked.

Now Angel Island is a beautiful park where you can hike, picnic, or camp. A good hike takes you to the top of Mt. Livermore, which is named for Caroline Livermore who helped make this island a state park. It is now home to wild-flowers, mule deer (who swam across from the mainland), and lots of raccoons.

The island was once the first destination of Asian immigrants to this country. You can visit the old quarantine hospital where sick people stayed to prevent the spread of contagious diseases.

The other island in the Bay is not so pretty or pleasant. In fact, the nickname for **Alcatraz Island** is "the rock" because it has no source of fresh water and only birds could live there. Yet

The ferry ride to Alcatraz takes only ten minutes. But as you pass over the cold, shark-infested water, think of the 39 men who tried to escape. Only five may have made it—that is, they were never seen again!

The word "Alcatraz" comes from the Spanish word for albatross.

this rock was first turned into a fort and then a federal prison. Alcatraz was "home" to 1,500 criminals such as gansters Scarface Al Capone and Machine Gun Kelly.

The prison is now a U.S. National Park Service Monument, where you can visit the cells of famous "guests" and see evidence of their desperate escape attempts. For instance, three inmates left behind "dummies'" made of bits of soap, cement, and human hair. Their trick fooled the guards long enough for a getaway.

Hopefully, this trip to Alcatraz will be the closest you come to entering a jail cell! It's a great place to visit but you wouldn't want to stay there—even overnight. So check the ferry schedule and don't get left behind.

Tickets for the ferry to Alcatraz Island are sold at Pier 41. They sell out quickly so buy early in the day or on the day before (Red and White Fleet, 546-2896).

9. The Hills—42 Ups and Downs

alfway up **Telegraph Hill** along the steep Filbert Street steps is a sign that reads, "I have a feeling we're not in Kansas any more."

Could that be Dorothy speaking to Toto in the *Wizard of Oz*? Why do you imagine Dorothy realizes she's no longer in Kansas? You guessed it. Kansas is almost totally flat; San Francisco is anything but. Altogether, there are 42 hills ranging in height from 200 to 938 feet. Some streets are so steep, just riding a car up and down can be pretty exciting. From the top it may seem as if your car is about to roll over backward. On the way up, you'll imagine your engine saying, "I think I can, I think I can . . ."

To prevent accidents, there are rules for parking: (1) curb wheels; (2) park in gear; (3) set brake.

Other rules are don't charge downhill in brand-new leather-soled shoes and don't open your car's downhill side door when a bag of oranges could fall out. Can you make up any other rules?

Some famous hills in San Francisco are:

Russian Hill—possibly named for the Russian immigrants who gardened here. Before California became a state, many Russians came here to hunt seals for fur. Since the territory became part of the United States, many Russian

When Isadora began, people thought ballet was the only form of dance. She shocked audiences by wearing a loose tunic and dancing in bare feet.

Lilli was a lifelong friend of San Francisco fire fighters. At age 15, she became the fire department mascot.

immigrants settled in San Francisco. Like the Chinese, Japanese, Hispanic, and other cultures, they brought their language, foods, and customs.

In some stores you can buy black bread, smoked fish, and other specialties. And you'll hear lively discussions in Russian.

Down one side of Russian Hill is **Lombard Street**, called the curviest street in the world. Brightly painted Victorian houses and beautiful flowerbeds border the street.

Nob Hill is named for the "nabobs" (a word for people of wealth and influence) who lived here. Tour the top to see their fabulous mansions. At the elegant **Fairmont Hotel,** you can enjoy an incredible citywide view while riding on the glass-walled elevator.

Isadora Duncan had a studio here at the beginning of this century. Called a pioneer of modern dance, she wasn't afraid to experiment and create entirely new ways of moving. Dance has never been the same since Isadora!

From the top of **Telegraph Hill**, people once watched for ships entering the harbor. At that time, San Franciscans depended on ships for everything—supplies, news, and visitors. When a boat was sighted, the exciting information was transmitted via telegraph to the rest of the city.

Also, from the top of Telegraph Hill, you'll see a 360 degree panoramic view of the city and the Bay. Do you recognize places you've been to?

To climb still higher, step inside the elevator in **Coit Memorial Tower.** It ascends 180 feet to an observation gallery.

Some say this tower looks like a fire hose nozzle. That would have pleased Lilli Coit. She gave the money for the tower to add "beauty to the city I have always loved."

10. Clowning Around and Carousels

an you imagine being ringmaster of a circus? Well, eleven-year-old Lorenzo John has that job. Of course, it may have helped that his father is a clown named Lorenzo Pickle (with size 72D shoes). As for his Mom, she helped found the fabulous San Francisco **Pickle Family Circus** where he works.

Ringmaster Lorenzo John is not the only kid in the show. Eleven-year-old Miriam Sela does a balancing act that keeps your eyes glued on the action. Lorenzo and Miriam perform a lot, and part of the money they earn goes for a good cause such as helping handicapped children.

If you yearn to learn how to perform, contact **Make-A-Circus**(Fort Mason Center, Bldg. C, 776-8477). Whenever this talented group performs, they hold workshops on circus skills for kids.

Do you know the biblical expression "turning swords into plough shares"? It means making something used for war into something useful. An example of this is the **Fort Mason Center**, an old army base that was turned into a cultural park.

San Francisco is famous for "street theater."

With so many clowns in town, it's no wonder San Francisco is home to the famous funny fellow Mork (Robin Williams).

34

Fisherman's Wharf and **Union Square** are especially popular for performers. You'll see jugglers, musicians, mimes, actors, and actresses performing on any sidewalk.

The looniest performance in town is **Beach Blanket Babylon**. Who can resist a singer who's wearing a complete pizza pie for a hat? Another huge hat might be a decorated Christmas tree or the San Francisco skyline!

Kids less than age 21 can attend Sunday matinees at 3:00 p.m. Call in advance for reservations. Tickets sell out fast. (Club Fugazi, 675 Green St. at Columbus; 421-4222)

San Francisco is sometimes known as *"Carousel City."* You can ride on lively painted camels, goats, deer, pigs, roosters, lions, and giraffes at old-fashioned merry-go-rounds at the **San Francisco Zoo**, **Pier 39** in Fisherman's Wharf, the **Children's Playground** in **Golden Gate Park,** and **Tilden Park** in Berkeley.

For thrills, spills, and laughs galore, find out when and where the Pickle Family Circus (587-8148) is performing.

*At the **American Carousel Museum,** 633 Beach St. (across from the Cannery at Fisherman's Wharf), watch as restorers fix antique hand-carved animals.*

11. Bridging the Bay

You can walk or bike across the Golden Gate Bridge.

Treasure Island is man-made. It was created for the 1939 World's Fair by dumping dredged earth on a very shallow part of the Bay.

Starring the Golden Gate Bridge

Age: Constructed 1933
Length: 8,981 feet
Weight: 495,000 tons
Width: 90 feet (6 traffic lanes and 2 sidewalks)
Height: As tall as a 65-story building above the water
Each cable contains 27,572 wires.

Before its construction, people said, "No way. . . it can't be done."

By doing it, Joseph Strauss (height: 5 feet) made engineering history. When first built, it was the longest single-span bridge in the world. To protect the workers, Strauss invented a safety net that saved many lives.

Co-starring the San Francisco-Oakland Bay Bridge

Length: 8 miles (the world's longest bridge over open water)
Height: 48 feet (a 4-story building could be towed beneath)

On the way, you pass two islands: **Yerba Buena** (once called Goat Island) and **Treasure Island**. Please, don't get too excited. This is not the home of Captain Hook, it's a military base.

12. Parks Aplenty

It's a good thing the early settlers landed on the East Coast; if they'd landed in San Francisco first, the rest of the country would still be uninhabited.

—Herbert Mye

If you stand on the bluff in Presidio Park overlooking the Bay, it's easy to pretend that you have arrived with the first band of settlers.

Imagine neither houses, bridges, nor roads before you. All you see are golden hills dropping down to sparkling blue waters, shady forests of tall evergreens, sunny fields of colorful wildflowers. Bird-filled marshes circle the Bay.

The waters of the Bay are filled with fish. Seals and sea lions bask on warm rocks. Birds soar past.

This beautiful setting has thrilled everyone who has come here. But, of course, as more and more people came, the landscape changed. As land was cleared for homes and businesses, much of the original wildlife (bears, wolves, condors) disappeared.

Dedicated individuals are working to preserve the beauty of this area for future generations. Laws have been passed to protect the marshes and to clean the waters. It is illegal to hunt seals, kill pigeons, or dig up native wildflowers.

Large chunks of land have been set aside for parks so people can quickly escape city life and find peace in quiet woods or on clear ocean beaches.

Gray whales are occasionally sighted from Land's End. They pass during long yearly migrations. These huge mammals travel nearly 10,000 miles in late fall from the Arctic to warm waters off the coast of Mexico. The return trip takes place during the early spring.

When whale watching, look for a spout of water above the waves. This is the whale exhaling its breath. The California gray whale is only medium size as whales go. Yet, it can measure 50 feet in length and weigh 40 tons.

Sutro was also concerned about the seals that lived nearby. To protect them from hunters, he helped create laws making the seals "citizens" of San Francisco.

One group of parks is called the **Golden Gate National Recreation Area,** or **GGNRA** (different from the **Golden Gate Park**). Part of GGNRA is a long narrow park that follows the coast around the peninsula.

The park, **Land's End,** is especially popular with hikers. While close to downtown, its rugged paths seem miles from any civilization.

South of Land's End is a famous bluff with a fabulous view. At the **Cliff House**, you can look down at the forceful Pacific surf crashing on rocks. You'll also see pelicans flap past, gulls dive, and barking seals sun themselves on **Seal Rock.**

In the last century, Arthur Sutro built a splendid glass bathhouse at the Cliff House. Thousands swam in the bathhouse in pools of ocean water mixed with warmer water. Years ago, it burned down. (You can still see its foundations at the ocean's edge.) But because of Sutro's efforts, the seals remain.

Water, water everywhere, but where can I swim?

While the Pacific Ocean looks beautiful, its cold waves and strong currents are very dangerous. Every year people are accidentally swept off the rocky coast and drowned. So be careful!

If you want a cool dip, **China Beach** (28th and Sea Cliff avenues) is a sheltered cove with calmer waves. The National Park Service provides changing rooms and a lifeguard during summer months.

You can reach other great GGNRA parks by crossing the **Golden Gate Bridge** into Marin County.

Mount Tamalpais presides over a setting of

golden hills and green woods. To the Miwok tribe, the slope of Mount Tamalpais looks like the form of a sleeping woman. They believe this is the figure of an Indian girl, loved by the sun god. When he tried to carry her away to his home in the sky, she fell from his arms. Now the maiden waits for him forever in the form of the mountainside.

A hike to the top of Mount Tamalpais (2,600 ft. above sea level) provides a spectacular ocean view. On a clear day, you can see mountain ranges, north, south, and east.

On the slopes of Mount Tam (as it is affectionately called) remains one virgin (never cut) stand of redwood trees. Coast redwoods, the tallest and oldest trees in the world, grew during the age of dinosaurs. Redwoods especially relish the fog that rolls over these hills. On the redwood branches, you may see drops of water condensed from the moisture in the air and known as "fog drip."

These giant redwoods are in a special park called **Muir Woods** (only 16 miles from San Francisco). Muir Woods is named for a famous American naturalist named John Muir. Born in Scotland, Muir traveled to the United States in 1849. He walked across half this country carrying only a penknife in his pocket. Muir camped out, winter or summer, using a pile of leaves for bedding. He spoke and wrote in favor of creating parks that preserved the rivers, mountains, and trees he so loved.

Discover other parks by crossing the San Francisco-Oakland Bay Bridge. On a high hill above the town of Berkeley, you'll find **Tilden Park** where you can ride on a steam engine train,

The tallest redwood now standing is 367 feet high (a football stadium is 300 feet). The oldest known redwood lived 4,000 years.

If you visit Mount Tam or Muir Woods, you're near the Marine Mammal Center (see chap. 13, Special Attractions for Animal Lovers). Try to find time to go to both places.

Check out the great Lawrence Hall of Science (see chap.13, Special Attractions for Science Nuts) in the center of Tilden Park.

The Children's Fairyland offers plays and puppet shows. Call 452-2259 for a schedule and fees.

an old-fashioned carousel, or a live pony. Other activities include picnics, boating, or swimming in lovely Lake Anza.

Lake Merritt in Oakland is surrounded by the 160-acre **Lakeside Park**. Since 1870, this has been a wildlife sanctuary (a protected space for animals and birds). It's the oldest in the United States.

From Lake Merritt just follow the Yellow Brick Road or tunnel through the Rabbit's hole in Alice in Wonderland. Either way you will discover **Children's Fairyland** and your storybook favorites such as Mother Goose, Billy Goat Gruff, and Pinocchio.

Nature is always near in San Francisco. And it's always worth the trip. You'll return refreshed to city sightseeing. And you'll understand why San Francisco draws people to visit again and again.

13. Special Attractions

Ever wonder where Mr. Wizard spends his vacations?

Call 563-7272 for reservations for the Tactile Dome.

or Science Nuts

Do you remember the kooky scientist's messy laboratory in *Back to the Future*? Ever want to visit it?

Get ready—because you're going to explore the **Exploratorium.** There's nothing quite like it in the world, and you may want to spend hours and hours there.

The Exploratorium started years ago when some artists and scientists got together and created "a museum of science, art, and human perception." The museum continues to change, with inventors trying out new possibilities all the time.

You know how in most museums everything looks perfect and there are signs everywhere saying, "Please Do Not Touch." At the Exploratorium, everything is a *mess* and every exhibit begs you to touch, adjust, and fiddle with it some more! All the while you're learning about light, language, fission, fusion, friction, vibration, oscillation, and more.

In the middle of the Exploratorium is something very *weird* called the **Tactile Dome**. Inside the dome, it's dark, completely—you can't see

Laser at the Exploratorium

For more information on Tilden Park, see chapter 12, Parks Aplenty.

The Lawrence Hall of Science was named for Ernest O. Lawrence. He was a Nobel Prize-winning physicist who invented the cyclotron. So what's a cyclotron?

anything, only *feel*. That's all you get to know in advance. Once inside—when *it's too late*—then you find out.

Reach for the stars. . . but first, cross the Bay Bridge and drive up, up, up to the **Lawrence Hall of Science**. It's located on a hill above Berkeley in the center of Tilden Park.

Count the sides—the building is octagonal, or 8-sided. Eight is the number of physical sciences: biology, geology, astronomy, physics, chemistry, nuclear science, mathematics, and space science.

How? Why? What if? Discoverers of all ages have always asked these questions and in searching for answers they have made great scientific progress.

Discover on your own in the Lawrence Hall of Science through microcomputers and automated games like the Habitat Tic Tac Toe. Check out a seismograph that records earthquakes worldwide. Create a light show with a laser. Attend a star show in the planetarium.

Also find out about the Biology Lab Workshop, where you can use a stethoscope to compare animal heartbeats. And look for the Wizard's Lab Workshop, which lets you experiment with solar energy, static electricity, and other phenomena.

For workshop labs, tickets are sold at the Information Desk on a first-come, first-serve basis. The planetarium and workshop labs have special schedules. Call 642-5134 for days and times.

Another good reason to cross the Bay is the **Oakland Museum.** There you'll find a fascinating exhibit on California ecology, the science showing the relationship of life to its environment. California is the third largest state and contains many different physical environments.

At the museum, you first get the total picture by seeing a landscape model of the state. Then, through the film *Fast Flight*, you'll get a bird's view, flying east from the ocean to vast deserts.

For close-ups, walk through the gallery and observe how climate, geography, and wildlife change from one zone to another. The soggy salt marshes support one kind of living community, while the redwood forest offers a completely different habitat.

Examine closely the food chain dioramas— each is a world, complete with animals, insects, reptiles, birds, plants, and fungi.

For a different adventure, cross the Golden

For an out-of-this-world view, take a break in the Galaxy Sandwich Shop (Lawrence Hall of Science). The food is definitely of this world: hot dogs, burritos, doughnuts, and other tasty stuff.

When in Oakland, do as Oaklanders do. Go to Fenton's Creamery (4226 Piedmont Ave.)—famous for huge ice cream concoctions! Plus freezes, floats, and fizzes.

Watch the dinosaur at the Lawrence Hall of Science—it moves!

Gate Bridge to Mill Valley and head for the **Bay Area Discovery Museum** in Corte Madera (428 Town Center, 927-4722). Here you can try out theories of art, architecture, mechanics, and drama through a variety of materials and activities. Call for a program schedule.

For History Buffs

On almost every page of this book, you'll find tidbits of history. That's partly because San Francisco has been around a long time. Also, the city has been home to many daring, imaginative people who in their lifetimes "made history."

Walking back in time is an adventure. Here are some stepping-off points.

The **Ferry Building** is a giant brick structure on the Embarcadero. Before the Golden Gate and Bay bridges were built, one hundred thousand commuters used to pass through here every day. Note the tall clock tower. It cracked during the San Francisco earthquake, so for one year the hands were frozen at 5:13 a.m.

You'll feel *vurry sophisticated* sipping a soda in the elegant tearoom of the **Sheraton-Palace Hotel** (on the corner of Market and New Montgomery). High above glitter crystal chandeliers and a glass-domed ceiling. Built in 1875, the Palace was known as the "grandest hotel in the world." Horse-drawn carriages entered the central glass-covered courtyard, and ladies in ball gowns stepped out, sheltered from wind or rain. The building, destroyed by the 1906 earthquake and fire, was rebuilt in 1909.

The **Wells Fargo Museum** (420 Montgomery St. at California) is part of a bank. That's not surprising considering all the gold coin Wells Fargo

Along the Embarcadero (this means dock in Spanish) oceangoing freighters are loaded and unloaded. Sacks of green coffee from South America, tea from Asia, English whiskey, French wines, Japanese cars—products arrive from all over the world. Then the empty ships cross the Bay to Oakland and fill their hulls with American wheat, corn, wood, and coal, which are carried overseas.

Can you figure out the reason a fort was put at this northernmost point of the peninsula?

stagecoaches carried cross-country. You'll see a stagecoach that actually made this trip. Plus pistols, photos, and gold nuggets.

Park Service rangers wear Civil War uniforms as they guide you through **Fort Point National Historic Site** (Presidio, reached via Lincoln Blvd. to Long Ave.; 556-1693). Not a shot was fired from this sturdy brick fort built just before the Civil War. Yet it was designed to mount 126 muzzle-loading cannon, and you can watch the daily cannon loading demonstration.

Cross the Bay Bridge, enter the **Oakland Museum,** and view a pageant of California history. From the Miwok and Costanoan Indian tribes to the Spanish colonial period. From the rough gold mining camps to luxurious Victorian era salons. From the ideal suburban kitchen of the 1940s to Hollywood's famous cartoon characters. You'll witness the stuff of daily life: tools, toys, clothes, utensils, weapons, machines—everything!

46

Oakland Museum

Start with the tule (reed) baskets and huts of the Miwok and Costanoan tribes that inhabited the San Francisco Bay area for thousands of years before settlers arrived from Mexico. Native Americans used the Bay—swimming to catch a fish and building rafts to travel. They ate shellfish, leaving piles of shells behind, which now show archaeologists where they lived. They also trapped animals and hunted with bow and arrow.

When settlers arrived, missionaries attempted to convert the Native Americans to Christianity. Some learned farming, weaving, and woodworking. They could not be protected, however, against disease and the despair of losing their own culture. Years later when the mission system was disbanded, few were left.

In the exhibit on the Spanish colonial era, you'll see leather saddles used by vaqueros (Spanish cowboys), embroidered shawls and decorated fans used by senoritas, and prayer books and retablos (holy pictures) that graced early mission churches.

The exhibit in the entire gallery spans a little over 200 years. Not much time when compared to the life of a redwood tree. Yet you'll be astounded by the quantity of artifacts (objects made by humans) packed into these displays!

History can be understood from the things that remain and also from stories.

In the beginning, a Costanoan legend tells, waters covered the earth except for the top of one mountain. On that mountain lived a coyote, a hummingbird, and an eagle. When the waters receded, these three creatures, but especially coyote, created the world.

As this legend indicates, animals are the co-creators of life. By revering even what is killed for food, a precious balance is maintained between human beings and the surrounding and supporting life.

For Animal Lovers

All sorts of cold-blooded and warm-blooded species inhabit the Bay area. While hiking you may encounter chipmunks, rabbits, skunks, gophers, turtles, toads, or snakes. (Only the Northern Pacific Rattlesnake is dangerous.)

Bird-watching is superb—many birds live here year-round. Gulls glide over the water. Egrets patrol the Bay marshes. Owls and kestrels hunt woods and fields.

If you visited **Cliff House** (see chap. 11, Parks Aplenty), you will have seen (and heard) the seals and sea lions that live there. These furry, warm-blooded mammals relish icy ocean water. The coast of northern California usually provides an ideal habitat. Yet, sometimes, water pollution, oil spills, or hunting result in their injury or death.

The **Marine Mammal Center** (Marine Headlands, Rodeo Beach, Fort Cronkhite, 331-7325) operates like the U.S. Coast Guard for sick or

Here is a true story from the Hispanic era of California. Where Oakland and Berkeley are located was once a 45,000-acre ranch. The owner, Don Luis Maria Peralta, was a very old man when the Americans claimed California in 1846. Two years later, gold was discovered and people went crazy. Shopkeepers left their stores; soldiers left their forts; farmers left their fields.

Don Luis was worried, so he called his four sons together, saying,"God has given this gold to the Americans. If He had wanted us to have it, He would have given it to us before this. So I tell you, do not go after it. Plant your lands and gather your crops. These are your gold fields for all must eat while they live."

What Don Luis said was true. For while gold mines made a few people rich, the farms of California have brought enduring wealth to this state.

Marine Mammal Center

Eleven different kinds of salamanders live in damp woodsy areas. Look around the edges of pools or streams. Salamanders resemble little lizards, but their skin is smooth and moist.

A 20-minute ride on the Zebra Zephyr train provides a quick introduction to the zoo.

injured seals and sea lions. When an animal is reported in trouble, someone investigates. Injured, orphaned, or diseased creatures are brought back for treatment. Once they are well and can take care of themselves, they are returned to the coast. At the Center, you can watch as animals are fed and healed.

To see lions and tigers and bears, visit the **San Francisco Zoological Gardens** (at the end of Great Highway at Sloat and Skyline blvds.; 661-6844).

There you can observe over 1,000 animals. These include 12 gorillas, a white tiger named Prince Charles, some pygmy hippos (who aren't much bigger than pigs), and a rare snow leopard.

You can watch the lions being fed between 2:00 p.m. and 3:00 p.m. every day except Mondays. They fast on Mondays.

Look for the Insect Zoo. It's full of your favorite bugs—spiders, beetles, scorpions, ants!

Gorilla World is the largest zoo habitat for gorillas in the world. You'll have a chance to view their antics from all different angles! Also find out what goes on at the Primate Discovery Center.

One of the best things about this zoo is that most of the animals are not stuck in cages. They are secure behind moats of water, yet they appear to be free and can move around a setting that resembles their home environment.

Next door is the **Children's Zoo,** which features baby animals. Through a window you may see a lion or lemur cub being bottle fed.

Across from the zoo is Leon's Barbeque (2800 Sloat Ave.; 922-2436). Chow down on barbecued ribs and chicken, baked beans or cole slaw. But try to save room for the little homemade sweet potato and pecan pies.

14. Hey Gang, I'm HUNGRY!

or *dim sum*, some good bets are the **Kow Loon Pastry** (909 Grant Ave., 781-7258) or the **Hong Kong Tea House** (835 Pacific, 391-6365). Count the little pastries you eat because the amount you pay is based on the number of plates stacked up at the end of the meal.

You know history doesn't stop 100, 25, or even 5 years ago. Today's history buffs will enjoy the music memorabilia at the Hard Rock Cafe (1699 Van Ness at Sacramento)—famous for milkshakes, fries, burgers, LOUD MUSIC, and a classic Cadillac on the ceiling!

For more about dim sum, see chapter 6, Close Neighborhoods.

Tengo hambre! There are many people of Mexican ancestry living in the **Mission District.** For some really wonderful tacos, visit **La Taqueria** (2889 Mission/25th St., 285-7117). This is a fast food restaurant where you can see what you're getting. Juicy chunks of meat, avocado, tomatoes, and cheese fill the soft corn tortillas. Many fruit juices are also available: strawberry, pineapple, cantaloupe and orange.

In the **Japan Center,** look for the **Mifune Restaurant** (922-0337). From the window, you can see a display of the different foods offered. All shown in little plastic models. Kids can get a plate called the "bullet train." This meal of noodles and *tempura* is served in a dish that looks like the super-fast Japanese train.

Tempura is made from vegetables and shrimp, dipped in batter and lightly fried.

Ho fame! The best thing about Italian restaurants is you can make a lot of noise and no one even notices. That's because everybody (cooks included) is truly yukking it up.

Everyone has a favorite Italian restaurant in San Francisco—and you may discover your own. Here are some popular choices where kids are welcome.

Little Italy (4109 24th St./Castro, 821-1515)— See the kitchen from the dining room, a glimpse of southern Italy. Do try to save room for the *zabaglione* for dessert—that's zah-bah-glee-oh-nee, a delicious custard.

Bertola's (4569 Telegraph Ave./Shattuck Ave. Oakland, 547-9301)—At this family-style restaurant, you may be seated at a long communal table. Lots of food for not a lot of money!

O Sole Mio (2031 Chestnut/Fillmore, 931-9008)—Pizza, pizza, pizza!

For a meal that is scrumptious and healthy,

You may discover that spaghetti made in a genuine Italian restaurant is very different from the spaghetti you ate at the school supper. And the pizza you get may not seem like Pizza Hut. But will your opinion be, "Oh no! It's different" or "Wow—how delicious!"? Depends on how flexible your taste buds are.

Jack London

visit **Greens Restaurant** (Fort Masons; 771-6222). It's all vegies and world famous for delicious food. (Also so popular your family must make reservations.) If you only want a snack, step inside the **Tassajara Bakery** in front for delectable breads and sweets.

Fat Apple's (1346 Grove/Rose, 526-2260) is a very popular place to eat in Berkeley. As American as apple pie or strawberry shortcake, everything here is made from scratch. On the walls are pictures of Jack London, the adventurous gold miner, oyster pirate, and journalist who grew up in this area.

15. Super Shopping Stops

ave you saved your allowance? You'll want to stretch your dimes and quarters as far as possible in San Francisco. No matter what direction you take, there are temptations galore. Try toys, for instance . . .

Ever been frustrated by toys that look good on the shelf but fall short once you get them home? You needn't fear that at **The Imaginarium**: A Toy Store Kids Can Handle (3535 California St., 387-9885, and 3251 20th Ave., 566-4111). At this California-based chain, it's positively "hands-on." You can try out any of the merchandise on the spot to see if it's *really* worth toting home.

HEFFALUMP (1694 Union Street at Gough, 928-4300) is also terrific for toys. Dolls, doll-houses, books, and art and music supplies—just tell your folks, *it's all educational!*

Do you think your parents ever played with toys? Most did and some even experienced the exquisite pleasure of a visit to **F.A.O. Schwarz** (180 Post St., 391-0100). This is the *granddaddy* of toy stores, so if a birthday or other significant event is on the horizon, take notes.

Have you noticed all the chic kids downtown? Where do they shop? The home base of **Esprit** (a

Levis are jeans—right? But where did the name come from? Levi Strauss was a peddler who arrived in San Francisco during the 1848 Gold Rush. He had lots of heavy tent canvas, but instead of making tents, he made pants. The many pants pockets were strengthened with metal rivets at the seams for holding tools.

Esprit, Illinois Street

trademark on clothes nationwide) is San Francisco. The outlet store (499 Illinois St. at 16th St., south of Market, 957-2550) has it all—shoes, socks, shirts, belts, bags, skirts, dresses, pants—at bargain prices. Mom or Dad will be pleased to know there are clothes in their sizes too.

Remember the all-time favorite bedtime story "Goodnight Moon" by Margaret Wise Brown? At **Land of Counterpane** (3610 Sacramento St., #A, in Presidio Heights, 346-4047) there's a room illustrated just like this book. In this bookstore aimed at kids, you can truly step inside the pages!

"Dungeons and Dragons" is just one of the games to explore at **Gamescape** (333 Divisadero

St., 621-4263). Card games, chess, Pictionary, darts—you name it—this store is stocked.

If you don't want a soggy suitcase, don't carry home a live fish. Still, you can look all you like. Thousands of exotic fish await your gaze at the **Nippon Goldfish Company** (3109 Geary Blvd., 668-2203).

Reach inside a water tank and choose an oyster. *It's guaranteed to contain a pearl* at the **Murata Pearl Company** (1737 Post in the Japan Center, 922-0666). And the pearl you find can be yours for about $7.00.

Look for the following among the many shops at Pier 39:

Left Hand World (433-3547) is a store devoted to the needs of "south paws."

San Francisco is known as the "kite capital of the world," and **Kitemakers of San Francisco** (956-3181) has a great selection. Look for ideas that can help increase the aerodynamics of your own model!

Puppets on the Pier (781-4435) specializes in—you guessed it—marionettes and puppets. Just imagine the fun shows you can direct back home with a new cast of characters.

16. Celebrating Round the Year

The seasons of the year are celebrated San Francisco-style. In festivals, fairs, and parades, the city's many cultures share their food, music, dances, and holiday customs. A few are listed here, but you can find out about others from local newspapers and magazines.

Meanwhile, around the city, nature enjoys its own rituals.

Each year, festivities begin with the **Chinese New Year** in late February or early March. A week of feasting and fireworks ends with a terrific parade on Saturday night, led by a dragon one block long. It takes 40 people to march it through the city.

Gray whales pass the coast heading north during their yearly migration.

Spring is welcomed in early April by the **Nihonmachi Cherry Blossom Festival** at the Japan Center. Dancing, drumming, and martial arts are demonstrated.

Sausalito was once a Portuguese fishing village. Now, the **Portuguese Chamarita Holy Ghost Festival** is held here on the Sunday six weeks after Easter with a parade and free sopa (soup) offered afterward.

In spring, a million songbirds twitter and trill while wildflowers carpet open spaces everywhere.

Dance, listen to music, and eat Hispanic food in the Mission District during the **Cinco de Mayo (May 5) Parade and Celebration.**

The **Fourth of July Celebration** goes sky high in Crissy Field with fireworks sponsored by the Golden Gate National Recreational Area.

During summer, warm days draw the fog across the land like a river of cotton.

In September, look for **KQED's Annual Ice Cream Tasting** at the Trade Show Center. Considered the world's largest ice cream extravaganza, money is earned for public TV!

The fall season is golden, the grasses dry; flocks of sea fowl pass on their way farther south.

An old Italian tradition, the **Blessing of the Fleet,** takes place on the first Sunday of October. A parade starting in North Beach heads to Fisherman's Wharf.

Rains begin and the dark gold gives way to a cool refreshing green as the year turns around.

The **Dickens Christmas Fair,** sponsored by the Living History Centre (892-0937), is held at **Pier 45** from the weekend before Thanksgiving through the weekend before Christmas. Victorian London is re-created—just imagine spending Christmas with Tiny Tim and Scrooge. Bah, humbug!

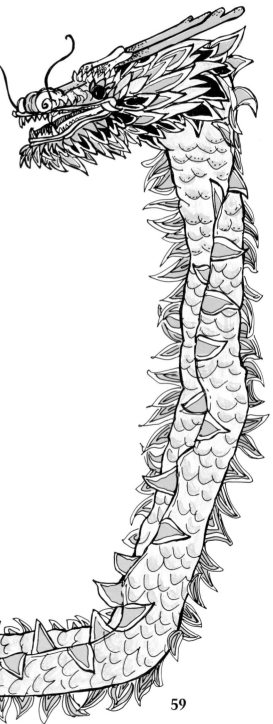

17. Fortune Cookies and Farewell

"San Francisco has only one drawback—'tis hard to leave."

—Rudyard Kipling

Write an "I will never again—" note for future travel plans.

When your best friend is figuring out a trip itinerary to San Francisco, what advice will you offer?

ave you discovered the truth in Kipling's statement? Oh, it's so hard to repack those bags, sticking in all the doodads and precious cargo you've collected.

And what about your head? Is it also packed with the sights, sounds, and smells of this fantastic city? Here are some more questions. What was most stupendous? Will you want to come back?

When you review your itinerary and think back on the trip, you may realize that some of the very best things that happened were unplanned. A friend gives you some tickets. A stranger points out a special sight. You happen upon a wonderful restaurant. No guidebook can prepare you for these delightful little surprises that arrive like fortune cookies at the end of a Chinese meal. And all you can say (to yourself) is "thanks."

One other thing you may realize, looking back, is travel is *not all fun*. You get stuck in traffic. You stand in a long, long ticket line and still you miss the last ferry ride—DRAT!

Happy travel means balancing the good with the not-so-good. Then putting it all behind you and planning for the next trip.

Index of Points of Interest

Alcatraz Island
Ferries depart hourly
beginning at 8:45 a.m.
from Pier 41; last boat
leaves island at 4:30 p.m.
Advance reservations sug-
gested during summer.
Red and White Fleet,
546-2896;
1-800-445-8880 in
California

**Cable Car Museum
Powerhouse and Car Barn**
474-1887, Washington
and Mason Streets
Open 10 a.m.-6 p.m. daily,
free

**California Academy of
Sciences, Aquarium,
Planetarium, and Natural
Science Exhibits**
Golden Gate Park
221-5100 or 750-7145
(tape)
Open 10 a.m.-5 p.m.,
Monday-Sunday

Admission charge; 1st Wed.
and Sat. (10 a.m.-noon),
free

**California Marine
Mammal Center**
Marin Headlands,
GGNRA (Fort Cronkhite),
331-SEAL
Open 10 a.m.-4 p.m., free

Children's Fairyland
1520 Lakeside Drive,
452-2259
Open daily, 10 a.m.-
5:30 p.m. (summer).
Call for schedule, other
seasons.
Admission charge

Chinese Culture Center
750 Kearney Street, 3rd
floor of Holiday Inn,
986-1822; open 10 a.m.-
4 p.m. Tues.-Sat., free

Cliff House
1090 Point Lobos between
Geary Blvd. and the Great

Hwy.; 386-1170
Open daily, free

Exploratorium
Palace of Fine Arts
3601 Lyon Street at
Marina Boulevard,
563-7337 or 561-0360
(tape)
Open 10 a.m.-5 p.m.
Wed.-Sun., admission
charge
1st Wed. of month and
every Wed. 6-9 p.m., free

Fort Mason Center
Laguna/Marina Boulevard
441-5706, 441-5705 (tape)

**Fort Point National
Historic Site**
Presidio of San Francisco
reached via Lincoln Blvd.
to Long Ave.
556-1693
Open 10 a.m.-5 p.m. daily,
free

GGNRA Headquarters—
Golden Gate National
Recreation Area
Fort Mason
556-3002

Hyde Street Pier
Foot of Hyde Street
Open daily: May-Oct.,
10 a.m.-6 p.m.; Nov.-Apr.,
10 a.m.-5 p.m.; free

Jeremiah O'Brien
Fort Mason, Pier 3, East,
Marina Blvd. and Laguna St.
441-3101; open 9 a.m.-3
p.m. daily; admission
charge
3rd weekend of month,
engines steam up

Lawrence Hall of Science
Centennial Boulevard,
Berkeley, 642-5133
Open daily 10 a.m.-
4:30 p.m.; Thurs. open
to 9 p.m.
Admission charge

**M. H. DeYoung Memorial
Museum**
Golden Gate Park
750-3600 or 750-3659
(tape)
Open 10 a.m.-5 p.m.,
closed Monday-Tuesday,
some holidays
Admission charge; 1st Wed.
and Sat. (10 a.m.-noon)
free

Mission Dolores
16th and Dolores Streets
621-8203; 9-4:30 p.m.
daily; admission charge

Morrison Planetarium
750-7140; Laserium Light
Shows 750-7183
1-hour daily sky show,
2 p.m. Monday-Friday;
weekends and holidays,
1, 2, 3, and 4 p.m.
Admission charge

Mount Tamalpais State Park
Panoramic Hwy, 15 miles
north via U.S. 101 (Mill
Valley)
388-2070, open 7 a.m.-
sunset

**Muir Woods National
Monument**
Golden Gate Headlands,
17 miles north via U.S.
101 and Hwy 1, 388-2595,
open 8 a.m.-sunset, free

Musée Mecanique (on
lower deck of Cliff House)
Collection of antique
mechanical and coin-
operated games
Admission charge

**National Maritime
Museum**
Aquatic Park at Polk and
Beach Streets

Oakland Museum
10 Oak Street
273-3401, 834-2413 (tape)
Open Wed.-Sat., 10 a.m.-
5 p.m.; Sun., noon-7 p.m.
Admission charge

**San Francisco International
Toy Museum**
The Cannery, 2801
Leavenworth, 441-TOYS
Open Tues.-Sat.
10 a.m.-6 p.m., Sunday
11 a.m.-5 p.m.
Admission charge

San Francisco Zoo
45th at Sloat
661-7777; 661-4844 (tape)
Open 10 a.m.-5 p.m. daily;
admission charge

Children's Zoo, 661-2023,
admission charge

Tilden Regional Park
Berkeley, park office
843-2137
Merry-Go-Round,
524-6283
Train, 531-9300
Pony Ride, 527-0421
Environmental Center,
525-2233
Call for hours; admission
charges

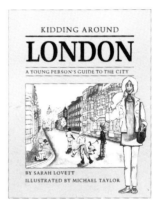